Don't Grown-Ups Ever Have FUN?

JAMIE HARPER

LITTLE, BROWN AND COMPANY

New York · An AOL Time Warner Company

For Lexi

Special thanks to my three supermodels,
Grace, Lucy and Georgia.

Copyright © 2003 by Jamie Harper

First Edition

Library of Congress Cataloging-in-Publication Data

Harper, Jamie.
Don't grown-ups ever have fun? / by Jamie Harper — 1st ed.
p. cm.
Summary: Things that are wrong with adults include wearing boring clothes,
refusing to share their stuff, and liking things clean.
ISBN 0-316-14664-1
[1. Growth — Fiction. 2. Behavior — Fiction. 3. Parent and child — Fiction.] I. Title.
PZ7.H23134 Wh 2003
[E] — dc21   2002022489

10 9 8 7 6 5 4 3 2 1

Printed in Mexico

Would you believe it? Mom and Dad are STILL in bed.

We don't waste time sleeping . . .

when there's a zillion things to do.

- OOOUCH!

As soon as they get up, it's rush, rush, rush.

Actually, we like to take it easy.
Poor Mom and Dad. Why can't they be like us?

Take Dad. He's so fussy.

He wears the SAME clothes to work every day.

We don't. We're always changing outfits.

Plus, he makes us watch boring TV.

We like shows you can see again and again.

Even his office is boring—all black and white.

Honestly!

Dad's not the only fussy one. Mom's picky about her stuff too.

All the time it's "Please don't touch."

C'mon, Mom, let's share!

She won't ever let us help her . . .

even though we're perfectly willing.

No wonder she says she needs to get away....

Silly Mom, we can take care of her right here at home.

Now look at them! Cleaning up's their favorite thing to do.

Why does it all have to be so perfect?

OH NO! Not our playroom too.

There, much better.

Mom and Dad should be more like us.

Would you believe it?

Well, I guess they used to be kids once too.